I'll Always Come Back!

by Steve Metzger • Illustrated by Joy Allen

SCHOLASTIC INC.

New York   Toronto   London   Auckland   Sydney
Mexico City   New Delhi   Hong Kong   Buenos Aires

To Nancy and Julia . . . always!
— S.M.

To Angela with love.
— J.A.

ISBN 0-439-42922-6

12 11 10   6 7/0

Printed in the U.S.A.
First printing, September 2002

ROOM 5

We go off to school,
say good-bye at the door.

Although I can't stay,
I'll always come back!

You play with your friends—
run, jump, and climb.

I look at your photo
when I'm at my desk.

Your teachers will help
if you fall and get hurt.
And when school is over,
I'll come back to you.

You listen to stories
of mice, stars, and trains.

I'll read to you later
when you're tucked in your bed.

You bake bread at school,
and sweet muffins, too.

We'll talk all about it.
You know I'll be back!

You love to paint pictures
of dogs, birds, and trees.

I draw at my table
while thinking of you.

When you play outside,
you dig down, down, down,
as deep as my love.
I'll always come back!

Your buildings with blocks
reach up to the sky,
just like my office
where I work downtown.

You make snakes and bunnies
with squeezable clay.
I can't wait to see you.
Yes, I'll be back soon!

Floor puzzles are fun
for you and a friend.
My friends help me, too,
when there's work to do.

You sit in a circle and sing favorite songs.

I love you so much, and . . .
I'll always come back!